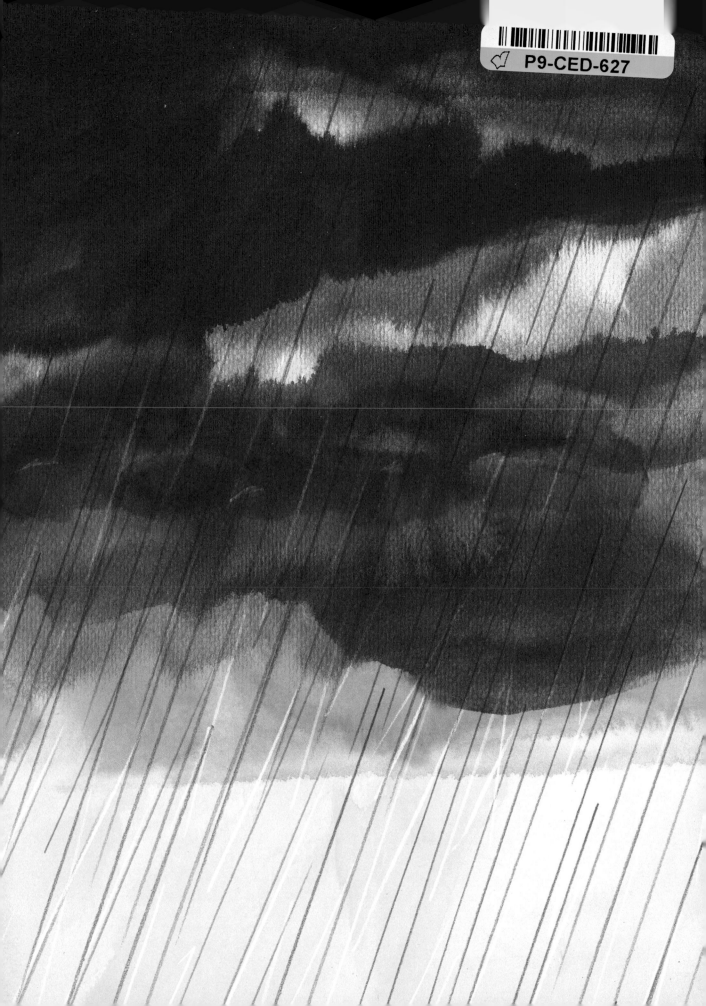

This Beautiful Day

by Richard Jackson

illustrated by Suzy Lee

A CAITLYN DLOUHY BOOK

ATHENEUM BOOKS FOR YOUNG READERS

New York   London   Toronto   Sydney   New Delhi

Thinking of
Robert J. Verrone (1934–1984),
and remembering the beautiful days of Bradbury Press
—R. J.

For my father
—S. L.

ATHENEUM BOOKS FOR YOUNG READERS
An imprint of Simon & Schuster Children's Publishing Division
1230 Avenue of the Americas, New York, New York 10020
Text copyright © 2017 by Richard Jackson
Illustrations copyright © 2017 by Suzy Lee
For information about special discounts for bulk purchases, please contact Simon & Schuster Special Sales
at 1-866-506-1949 or business@simonandschuster.com.
The Simon & Schuster Speakers Bureau can bring authors to your live event. For more information or to book an event,
contact the Simon & Schuster Speakers Bureau at 1-866-248-3049 or visit our website at www.simonspeakers.com.
Book design by Debra Sfetsios-Conover
The text for this book was set in Pinch.
The illustrations for this book were rendered in pencil and acrylics and digitally manipulated.
Manufactured in China
0517 SCP
First Edition
2 4 6 8 10 9 7 5 3 1
CIP data for this book is available from the Library of Congress.
ISBN 978-1-4814-4139-1
ISBN 978-1-4814-4140-7 (eBook)

THIS beautiful day . . .

has everyone dancing

and spinning

and swinging

around,

has all of us stamping

and stomping
our feet
on the ground. . . .

This beautiful day . . .

has all of us skipping

and singing
and calling
aloud

or whistling

and whooping

enough for a crowd. . . .

This beautiful day . . .

so great for parading,

for cartwheeling fun

or hiding

and seeking

or gliding

and sliding
in this marigold sun,

high-fiving

and yes,

we're-alive-ing,

teetering-

tottering

everyone

clapping

even toe tapping

napping at last,

then . . . snacking—
doodly (slurp),

doodly (burp),

doodly-doo and doodly-dee.
All together, oh yes,

in this perfect weather

on this beautiful day.

Oh say can you say

this bea-u-ti-ful day?